Dedication

To Skye, George and Gabriel and all the future Nicol's
that come along.

Introduction

Have you ever found yourself wondering what happens to the mysterious disappearance of lost socks? Her lost sock, His lost sock, YOUR lost sock!

Ask your parents this puzzling question and the answer is quite frankly always the same!

"I just don't know where they go, a pair goes into the washing machine and every now and then, one sock simply disappears!" says Mum.

Dad scratches his head and smiles. "Yes, it's a funny thing, I'm still looking for my lucky sports sock I had lost back in 1989 after winning the one hundred metre sprint!" proudly tapping his chest.

Mum interrupts, "Yes, dear, but I don't think you would be quite as quick these days?"

"Ah," says Dad laughing! "That's because I've lost my lucky sock!"

There are trillions of stories such as this the world over. Every home has one and, in some cases, several.

Well, I will let you into the best kept secret of ALL TIME!

Prepare yourself, for I am about to tell the tale of the secret society of socks. A tale that will both excite and shock whoever is bold enough to read on!

Are you ready? Did I hear you say YES? And you honestly believe in our very existence? Then our story begins.

Allow me to introduce myself! My name is Sterling Sox.

Once a regular size 3 lucky sport sock, the day had come when I would be transported to the metropolis of Soxville. Let me explain my journey!

Chapter 1
SOAP AND SUDS

It was just another washing day, or so I thought! Just another day of swirling through the soapy waters of the machine that my keeper, Gabriel, had insisted his mother would suitably rewash his lucky sock, 'Me', once again!

I have been Gabriel's lucky sport sock for a long time; a skiing accident that year had broken his other foot and my twin had vanished. I had almost forgotten we were once a happy pair!

But this would be the day that I would remember forever. This would be a journey I could never forget.

Inside the washing machine, soap suds and other laundry tossed and turned. Dizzy and covered in bubbles, suddenly I found myself falling through a trapdoor!

Lights began to flicker with just enough light to see, and to my amazement I was sat inside a carriage. An announcement indicated that travel was expected, so I buckled up as quickly as I could.

Strange siren noises echoed within, and like a bullet I was transported to another dimension. With hardly enough time to catch my breath the door flew open.

A travellator quickly spat me out in front of a huge dryer, where two mechanical hands fitted me with a rather dapper outfit.

I must confess after catching a glimpse in the mirror looking smart, I gave myself a wink and grinned! A nano second later the exit door opened, so I decided to step through!

Chapter 2
THE THREE SLEUTHS

"Good afternoon, we have been expecting you, Agent Sterling!"

Three mysterious figures, all with perfectly matching groomed hairstyles, were there to greet me!

"Let's walk and talk; I shall explain everything along the way!" clarified one.

Glancing over I read the name tags poking out of their over-sized jackets.

Sleuths Steele, Scissor and Stone!

I listened intently as to how my arrival had been long awaited and it was the three sleuths' job to keep my mission TOP SECRET.

They went on to explain I would be strictly undercover.

Boggled, as I assumed it was a case of mistaken identity, Sleuth Stone assured me that I would be debriefed about the mission back at Headquarters.

Stepping outside, Steele opened the door of a strange looking mode of transport.

"This is another brand auto capsule in case you are wondering? I am sure you are familiar with the popular children's TV show that explores the many uses of a top selling washing up liquid bottle. This one has been censored! It happens to be Soxville's most sort after recycling item. It's amazing how many things you can make from each bottle, It's our favourite TV show, Purple Peters!" Sleuth Steele continued.

I smiled and replied, "Soxville?"

Together Steele, Scissor and Stone announced, "This is Soxville. Welcome to Soxville!"

Chapter 3
SCOTLAND YARN HQ

I gazed in curiosity as we hurried along. The streets were brightly coloured like an artist's pallet, and everything seemed to be made of wool and fabric.

Rivers, buildings, animals – all handmade. Rubbing my eyes in surprise, was I possibly dreaming?

Suddenly, we stopped to a halt right outside a building that read New Scotland Yarn HQ.

Taking a deep breath, I knew this was real. Stepping out of the auto capsule I headed towards the Headquarters.

Once inside I was greeted by the roaring sound of applause. Looking around, a large group were cheering and clapping at my arrival.

"Welcome, Sterling Sox, we have been expecting you for quite some time," announced a curious character!

"I'm General Ponsonby Smythe," he added.

Looking at the General with wide eyes, he was an unusual fellow with lots of medals which, on closer inspection, appeared to be made of milk bottle tops.

Intrigued to learn more! "Pleased to meet you, sir, how can I be of service?" I replied.

It was not long before I was told the whole tale and was updated with the current situation.

The instinct that Strider, my lost twin, was still out there somewhere was right!

It had been explained that Strider, now known as Swag, was Soxville's number one outlaw.

Swag's motley crew of misfits was Coalstone Jack, Jigsaw, Snitch, Ssssirus and Pongo. All of which had been creating mischief and my mission, if I choose to take it, would be to track down Swag's hideout.

The General had suggested I would know where he may be hiding because we were once a pair and think alike.

Chapter 4
THE GANG'S ALL HERE!

The very next day I awoke with such a jump. Fluff was shouting in my ear!

"Get up, rise and shine!" he hollered.

Who is Fluff, I hear you ask? Sorry for the late introduction! Let me explain!

Fluff and I have been acquainted since my first wash day!

Brave, witty and the brains of the outfit, well at least Fluff would like to think he is! Inseparable we make a great team.

A tad shy, Fluff lives in my hair and whispers in my ear whenever he has something to say!

Which is usually a lot, I must say!

Fluff gathered his thoughts, looked me right in the eye and said, "No time for napping, let's go find the misfits!"

We had learned that the misfits were Swag's posse, who had all been sucked up in the drains of various washing machines and had all settled here in Soxville. Outcast, they formed an alliance and Swag was their chief.

Jigsaw, the comedian of the bunch; Snitch, a tumble dryer ball who loves to eavesdrop; Ssssirus, an adder snake who never leaves Swag's side; Pongo, a smelly sock monster; and last, but not least, Coalstone Jack, a witty Welsh coal pirate who insists he is the direct descendant of Captain Morgan. All are fiercely loyal to Swag.

I figured Fluff and I made a good team, but we would have to get creative if we were going to find the misfits!

Busting to have a good look around Soxville, I decided an old fashioned explore was needed.

Chapter 5
THE WALKABOUT

Fluff had suggested that the best way to get to know a place is to walk the land and streets, and of course he was right!

Soxville was a place like no other. Brightly coloured eye-catching buildings and homes in every direction.

The main square had a path that led you in a circle to an assortment of shops. As we passed, I shyly peeked through one – the window had THE NEEDLE BOX etched on the pane.

"Good morning, monsieur, welcome to my fashion house; my name is Madame Grande Dame Darning!"

Madame Darning, a flamboyant Parisian with many talents in the fashion industry, is one of Soxville's most interesting residents.

Darning has a reputation for being well respected, not just for her fabulous dresses and gowns she designs, but also for her insistence on good behaviour practice. The young ones who dare to be cheeky, rude or, worse, potty mouthed around Darning know what to expect!

Madame Darning sews up the mouths of the naughtiest until they have learned their lesson. Needless to say (excuse the pun) they usually learn quick!

Originally from Paris, Darning is an intriguing figure with specs that sit on the tip of her nose and I had heard that her walking cane transforms into a needle. I could see why the young ones were wary of her but I for one, thought Madame Darning was charming, even if Fluff did not think the same.

We chatted for a while, took a few notes of interest, thanked Darning for her time and made good our escape.

Outside, the ladies waved from the Button and Bows hair salon, we quickly skipped past the Pin Cushion Club and made our way towards Soxville's Taylor Made Inc and A Stitch In Time Esc.

Taylor Made Inc is a mega factory where all things in Soxville are produced and made. Buildings, furniture, roads, trees, just about everything really, all under one roof. A magical place that upcycles and recycles, but most importantly, Taylor Made Inc's most precious product is the infant sock. On the first Tuesday of every month happy pairs visit the Sox nursery and collect their new addition to the family.

Stitch In Time Esc I had discovered was a scientific conservatory that is TOP SECRET. However, I have it on particular good authority that basically, all new gadgets that are made are tested here and if passed, go on to be built in Taylor Made Inc.

Soxville was full of colourful buildings, boutiques and homes, but nothing as grand as the palace for the Toe of State royal residence, King Hoof of Soxville. Delighted to have been sent an invitation to the palace,

King Hoof had requested my attendance for dinner, and had kindly insisted that the littlest toe of the left foot of the palace be our room for the night.

Fluff had remarked that it was great to have somewhere decent to stay. It must be said that Fluff is extremely hard to please, but secretly I had hoped that the palace was as grand as I had imagined.

Chapter 6
HOOF PALACE

As the grand gateway of the palace doors opened, I became blinded by a flood of golden light. "Wow!" I murmured!

"Hope you packed well? We are staying!" said Fluff.

I looked around in amazement. The main hall was laden head to toe in gold. A majestic staircase spanned out to greet us, which led to the palace state room. On closer inspection I could see the gold was an assortment of mosaic bottle tops, glistening.

"Thrifty!" remarked Fluff.

"Resourceful!" I clarified, laughing.

As we gathered pace with each step of the staircase, I could feel the butterflies in my stomach. I must say I was rather nervous about meeting King Hoof. Suddenly, footman Hobble stated our arrival.

"Ah perfect, Agent Sterling come on in and take a seat!" King Hoof boomed.

His Majesty was a jovial figure who wore a crown always and even to bed, I was told.

King Hoof retold tales of Swag and the misfits, and all the wrong doings in his once happy kingdom.

"I assure you, your Majesty, I will get to the bottom

of this!" I cried. Following swiftly, I pledged allegiance to the crown.

"I knew I could count on you, Agent Sterling! Now let's eat!" declared the King.

Fluff had been buzzing in the king's ear for a good five minutes, making suggestions of hunger and filling his thoughts with scrumptious desserts; his patience had paid off and now His Majesty was licking his lips and making quick hand gestures to Hobble to make haste with our dinner.

I gave Fluff one of those miffed looks of disapproval, but really, I was glad as I was suitably famished myself.

King Hoof was exceptionally good fun and most entertaining. Holding court is his favourite duty and I'd say His Majesty had a heart of gold to match his bling palace, but as we laughed at all his best jokes, I had to remind myself we were there for a reason. We were there for a mission and that mission was about to begin.

Chapter 7
CLOG WOODS

"Tally Ho!" murmured Fluff as we sped up the path. A good night's sleep at the palace had given us the strength to get the mission underway.

After discussing tactics, it had been decided that we should investigate an area of importance that had possibly been overlooked.

Grand Dame Darning had mentioned that some unruly junior socks had been building forts in the woods, and had seen Pongo in the trees moving about trying his best to scare them.

Pongo was a great decoy for the misfits. Unlike the junior socks, who have no sense of smell until adulthood, the socks usually run away from the terrible smelly odours coming from Pongo; this in turn allows the rest of the crew to go about their naughty business.

However, this particular day it was noted that George and Charlie Legwarmer had followed Pongo into the woods for a clearer look. The pair had both spied Ssssirus and Coalstone Jack crossing the path. Knowing they should not be too far away from home, they ran back as fast as they could and told their not so happy parents of what they had seen.

The path to the woods, all the colours of the rainbow, suddenly came to an end.

Low and behold, the shoe tree woods spanned out before our very eyes. Gingerly, we tiptoed through the woods, hearing whispers!

Suddenly, a branch came down to greet us. "Welcome to Clog Woods!"

Startled, I turned around full circle; together, the shoe trees all began to sing and as we began to walk through, we were spurred on by the shoe trees.

Fluff commented it had been the best concert ever and that he had once been to Woodstock in the '60s. I thought maybe that was a slight exaggeration, but I would have to take his word for it, I was a sock of the '80s, besides it was all sock and roll to me!

Looking at my notes I concluded that we had arrived at the location of the secret den. Fluff had noticed a strange whiff in the air. Was it Pongo again, I thought?

Excited, could we possibly be that lucky we were closing in on the misfits? I must admit I was shaking like a leaf but determined to take a closer look.

Fluff was right – the air did have a certain pong to it.

"Follow the smell!" Fluff suggested.

I started to sniff, sniff, sniff, and sniffed as hard as I could. And there it was, an old tatty faded sock dangling on a branch.

Pongo was a creature made of several old smelly discarded socks, basically a sock monster, would you believe.

"I can only conclude that this here sock came from Pongo!" I announced.

"Really? Do you think so? I do wonder about you sometimes!" Fluff added with a hint of sarcasm.

OK, maybe it was obvious I smiled, but after all I was new to being an agent and I did have a lot to learn.

Combing through the area looking for clues, we were satisfied that little else was there of great importance, so we decided to set up camp and wait under the cover of darkness in case the misfits showed up.

It took a while for Fluff to get over the disappointment of not being wined and dined at King Hoof's palace that night, but he did agree it was a great idea.

I volunteered to take the first watch during the stakeout but as the sun went down and the Clog Woods shadows deepened, I wondered if a daytime stakeout would have been a better option.

Swag and the misfits were slippery customers who were experts at hide and seek, so a bit of creative thinking was needed in order to catch them.

I twitched at the sounds of the woods' night creatures. I was not entirely sure what the noises were or by what, but I did know that I had to stay alert, keep watch and listen for any action.

I must stay awake, I told myself, but as my eyes grew tired and blurry, I yawned away, thinking what would I say to my long-lost twin? Was Swag as mischievous and naughty as I was led to believe? In fear of falling asleep I awoke Fluff, after all we had agreed on keeping watch in turns.

It seemed that I had not even closed my eyes for long when Fluff suddenly became overly excited and began jumping up and down in my hair!

"Here they come, here they come!" Fluff called out.

Rubbing my eyes in disbelief, in the far distance I could see Ssssirus leading, closely followed by Coalstone Jack, Snitch and Jigsaw. A few seconds later a dark shadowy figure emerged.

"Could this be Swag?" I asked Fluff.

"Most definitely, I love an undercover stakeout!" Fluff whispered.

Truth was, this was our first and as the misfits grew closer, I gulped and quickly thought out our next plan of action.

Suddenly, a beam of light came through the woods in the other direction. Three figures appeared: sleuths Steele, Scissor and Stone.

"We thought you could do with some help?" the three explained.

Taking a big breath of relief, I then greeted them with a big smile and replied, "I'm glad to see you three, we have the misfits in our sights!"

Fluff, to be fair, had been shouting in my ear trying his best to get my attention!

"OK what is it?" I asked.

"The misfits and Swag, they have disappeared!" Fluff added.

I looked into the dark night; Fluff was right, it was just the five of us left. We had missed our big opportunity. The misfits had fled.

Chapter 8
THE BIG IDEA!

It had been decided that we should regroup at Scotland Yarn HQ the very next day.

We sat around the table discussing further lines of enquiries. I looked through all the evidence that the sleuths had gathered on the misfits.

"Ah ha! I have an idea!" Fluff whispered excitingly.

No one catches sight of Fluff because he is shy and exceedingly small – he is positively incognito.

This, of course, suits me, especially as when he has something brainy to say, I claim the idea as my own, so I was most intrigued as to what Fluff had to say.

Fluff pointed out that after looking at the map of Soxville he noted where most of the misfits activities had taken place.

"You can estimate an area of importance where the crew may be hiding based on the rule breaking locations!" Fluff murmured.

"Fascinating, and hopefully make me sound like a genius!" I added.

Naturally, I had HQ hanging on my every word. I ran through our plan to help find Swag's lair. After a short pause of silence my proposal was met with loud applause.

General Ponsonby Smythe stepped forward. "Well done, Agent Sterling, splendid idea, bravo!"

Whilst I was happy to take the credit for the plan, I knew I would have to make it up to Fluff another time, but for now, I was loving the limelight!

Pointing to an area on the map, I announced we needed to look the other side of Clog Woods from over the top of Mercy Mountain. Somehow, I could feel this was the place, the place I would have a secret hideout.

Swag was after all my twin and we had once upon a time been a pair; we thought the same, played and laughed together, but, of course, I could be wrong, but we would soon find out.

"Let us put this theory to the test!" I said confidently.

A lot was riding on this hunch, so I really hoped I was right!

Chapter 9
SEA OF PLENTY OF BAD WORDS

The special socks of the SBS would be accompanying us during our voyage to Mercy Mountain.

The crew socks sailboat is an impressive vessel I must say, all rigged out with all the bells and whistles, hard to believe that it was once a dish washing bottle.

As we set sail, I was giddy with excitement. My eyes grew bigger and bigger as I noted that the sea was formed from pages of books, and from time to time a random word would float by.

I was intrigued to hear the notion that negative words spoken would float to the sea. The sea of plenty of bad words would be a memorable voyage – still, I wondered what was waiting for us on the other side.

It was not long before Fluff's words of wisdom were being whispered. "Mmm, sea of bad words? Words are not bad? It's just the order and attitude they are spoken that make them less appealing!" Fluff added.

I quickly reminded him of Madame Darning's choice of discipline in order to keep the junior socks from being rude.

"That seems like an awful lot of effort – why can't they just fit every new-born with a zip instead, that way they only have to zip it closed when they like!" Fluff laughed.

"A zip!" I cried. "Why didn't I think of that? The Stitch in Time designer will be overjoyed with our creativity; I will have to mention it next visit!" I sniggered.

As we bobbed up and down on the sea of bad words I was feeling a tad green.

"Sea sickness is very common don't you know; I blame all those bad words!" Commando Tomo said.

"How so?" I asked.

"It's all those parents out there saying things like I'm sick and tired of you not listening to me – all those negative words end up out here!" Tomo scoffed.

I wasn't sure if we were on the same page but what I did know was that I was feeling very queasy and would have to take his word for it (excuse pun 2)!

"Land Ahoy!" I heard someone cry.

"Oh, wonderful, not long now and we will be back on terra firma!" Fluff announced.

Bobbing up and down on the Sea Of Plenty Of Bad Words had not been kind to him either so we both breathed a sigh of relief when we docked at Port Mercy.

Chapter 10
PORT MERCY

Port Mercy was a busy thoroughfare with lots of hustle and bustle. Several ships were docked here and Soxville was the next destination for most, but others were scheduled to go further afield. As one boat cast off, I heard the captain announce, "All aboard to Whirlpool Ally!"

I had only seen a map of Soxville, so I was intrigued to learn there were other places to explore.

I had enjoyed the time getting to know the Special Commando Socks during our voyage. Some interesting tales were told. I was lucky to be in the company of some very brave socks.

Commando Tomo had relayed an historic mission that, under the cover of darkness, he had abseiled down a pipe to cut open a laundry bag to help three VIP socks to escape.

It had been a mission full of risks and bravery; Tomo disclosed it was sleuths Steele, Scissor and Stone who had been rescued.

"That doesn't surprise me, those three couldn't fight their way out of a paper bag!" laughed Fluff.

I did think that was a tad harsh but, there again, maybe he did have a point!

A small task force of five, plus myself, made an equal number to the misfits' crew of six. We did, of course, have Fluff as a bonus so perhaps a sneaky advantage.

We were all issued with a backpack full of supplies needed for the journey. As we made haste up the path leading towards Mercy Mountain, I did wonder if that extra pair of underpants was necessary. My bag was beginning to feel heavy already, but it would be a while yet before we would make it to camp, so I'd best dig in I told myself!

Mercy Mountain was the other side of Clog Wood, so the idea was to surprise the gang by going the long way around the mountain. Swag would not expect this and hopefully will be caught off guard.

This was, of course, if the secret den was situated somewhere on the map. I guess only a few sightings and a strong hunch were all we had to go on, but I was sure I was right!

Mercy Mountain lived up to its name, a giant scary foreboding range of mountains.

I had been debriefed what to expect, but in the cold light of day my instinct was to run and head back to port!

Commando Tomo stepped forward and affirmed, "Show Mercy respect and compassion and she will let you pass!"

As we grew closer to the mountain base, storm clouds gathered and we stopped to put on an extra layer. Looking at the summit it was a long way off, so it was time to really pull my socks up!

It would take some time but as we neared the summit, I could feel the ground move. Quaking in my boots I quickly shut my eyes and covered Fluff's.

"Who goes there?" boomed a voice.

With one eye open I looked up. After introductions all round I explained that we needed to pass in order to complete our mission.

We were told that Mercy will not let just anyone pass, so we all had our toes crossed hoping she would.

"Mmm, I'm very picky who I choose to cross, you must respect the environment!" Mercy pondered.

Assuring Mercy we would all be highly respectful and that we certainly would not dream of littering, I boldly took a step closer and nodded to Tomo and his comrades.

"Not so fast, Agent Sterling!" Mercy screeched.

"I have a riddle for you – get it right and I will allow you to pass!" Mercy added.

After quite some time clearing her throat, Mercy continued.

"I am something socks like to climb, but I'm not a tree with branches!

"I have lots of snow at my summit, so beware of avalanches!

"What am I?"

I swiftly looked around – there was a lot of head scratching, followed by lots of umming and ahhings! I could feel sweat beads bounce off my forehead; the clock was ticking!

"Mercy Mountain!" screamed Fluff.

"Yes, we know her name!" I added.

"No, you dope, that's the answer, silly," Fluff sniggered.

"Mercy Mountain, Mercy Mountain!" I bleated.

"Splendid, Agent Sterling, you may pass; but remember the rules of my mountain and keep your litter, take it home!" she repeated.

As we looked behind and waved goodbye, I could not help but think Mercy was not that frightening. Respect was the deal, and we would have to keep that promise!

The mountain path was steep and craggy.

"Single file!" ordered Tomo.

Fluff peered over my hair to take a closer look.

"Crikey, it's a big drop to the valley below; take it easy and watch your step, now is not the time to be clumsy!" Fluff added nervously.

It has to be said, on numerous occasions I have tripped, slipped or slid, catapulting poor Fluff to many a bumpy landing, so I did get the sudden concern! I promised to be extra careful and refrained from laughing at the thought of my side kick flying through the air like Super Dust.

Of course, Fluff was right, we would have to be watchful and alert as we marched down the trail to the valley below.

Chapter 11
BOBBIN MAN

Bobbin Valley was bright and colourful. Every shade in the rainbow covered the land as far as the eye could see. Mostly discarded bobbins dominated the valley. High Top Forest and Clog Woods were visible from the other side of the river, so I knew we were in the right area and that we couldn't be too far from our goal. As we hiked through the forest of bobbins it suddenly became very dark.

"Who turned off all the lights?" Fluff asked.

Looking up I realised we were cloaked by a large shadow; actually, the biggest shadow that I had ever seen. What was behind it? Dare I look? I could already hear the gasps coming from the Special Sock Commandos with mouths wide open. I gulped – this would need courage!

"It's Bobbin Man, I thought he was a myth but he's the real deal!" cried Tomo.

Bobbin Man, at least ten bobbins high, towered above us! My knees started to shake furiously. Fluff, realizing we were in a difficult spot, suggested that we all just be friendly!

"Hello. Lovely day for a stroll!" I squeaked.

"Are you lost?" Bobbin Man boomed.

"Lost?" I questioned, slightly confused!

"I don't get many visitors come through here, so I figured you may be lost?" Bobbin Man added.

"Oh, I see, well no, actually we would very much like to explore the valley?" I replied.

"But only if it is OK with you, Bob?" I added.

"Who's Bob?" Bobbin Man asked.

Scratching my head, even more confused, I enquired, "Isn't that your name?"

"Me? Oh, no, my name is Randolph Floyd Wordsworth, actually; sorry, I should have introduced myself earlier, call me Wordsworth!"

"Sorry, I should not have assumed your name was Bob!" I sniggered.

We exchanged a few chuckles then set off down the path together with the Commandos following closely behind.

Wordsworth, large in stature with a big personality, was remarkably interesting, swapping funny stories; we laughed away the hours.

Wordsworth had been the perfect host and not wanting to outstay our welcome it was time to move on.

It had been a lonely existence for Wordsworth, well-read and jolly, Wordsworth I felt would make a great teacher. I proposed that Bobbin Valley would make an ideal location for a summer camp if he was happy with the idea!

"Overjoyed, my dear Sterling!" Wordsworth responded.

I promised to make suggestions to the Knee-high College on my return.

Having revealed my plans for our mission, Wordsworth hinted that we were on the right track and spoke of a crossroads that may be of interest.

"We should keep our eyes peeled!" I told the troops.

Heading down the path I felt pangs of excitement, were we really closing in on Swag and the misfits?

Chapter 12
THE CROSSROADS

It wasn't long before we reached the crossroads. Three choices lay before us – which one should we take?

Standing there looking at the options, Commando Tomo noticed that the crossroads had a post with a spinning arrow.

"How fascinating, give it a spin, Tomo!" I cried.

Tomo gave the arrow a good spin; around and around it spun until it stopped on the marker. A red big toe pointed towards the red path to the right.

We all agreed that it was a game of chance and that the red path was as good as any, so we decided to give it a go.

"Red route it is, let's do this!" I beamed.

"If it's the wrong choice then we would likely be doing a lot more walking!" Fluff muttered.

And of course, as per usual, he was right, but no one really knew where this path would lead us, so we would just all have to find out in good time.

Red route was aptly named. Everything was coloured red! Commando Tomo echoed to his troops to be on high alert and that it was a code red operation. I was waiting for Fluff to say something smart, but I guessed his silence was down to him being busy on lookout himself.

Suddenly, in the clearing ahead we could see what looked to be a giant puzzle on the ground; speeding up our pace we went for a closer look.

"Interesting, what do we have here then? I do believe it's some sort of crossword puzzle. I'm particularly good at solving these, often I play when reading the Soxville Times!" Tomo added.

"What an intriguing place to find a puzzle, don't you think?" Fluff whispered.

Laid out before us was a grid with six letters attached to a word.

"Mmm, let me see, we have a C S S P J and another S and an A to work with!" I declared.

S

W   P

COALSTONEJACK

G   N   N   I

I   G   G

T   O   S S I R U S

C   A

H   W

Set aside was a collection of letter tiles in disarray. We all set to work to solve the puzzle, mostly laughing at all the different combinations of words we could come up with.

A pattern suddenly emerged spelling out the entire names of Swag and the misfits. We were sure to be on the right track now weren't we, I thought!

Just then a golden magpie circled above us. Commando Tomo beckoned the bird!

"This is Memo, our carrier magpie!" he introduced.

"I do believe she has a message for us!" Tomo added.

Gingerly opening the note attached to her leg, it read, 'SOS SBS needed back at the palace, crown jewels stolen!'.

"Sorry, Agent Sterling, looks like we are needed pronto, you will have to fly solo on this mission I'm afraid, good luck!" Tomo cried.

Within seconds, the SBS were out of sight travelling back to the palace.

"OK, well it's just you and me, Fluff!" I murmured.

We looked across the valley in search of something, anything, that would lead us to new clues as to the whereabouts of Swag's den.

Fluff had seen something unusual under an old Clog tree that looked out of place. We marched towards a black and white path just ahead of us. On closer inspection we could see it was a piano keyboard that wrapped around an old box filled with cotton reel spools. I couldn't help but think this was the place we were looking for. After all, it was awfully close to the spot Fluff had marked on the map.

"X marks the spot!" Fluff remarked, beaming with pride.

Instinctively, I started to jump up and down on the keys; with delight it made a tune with every step. Chopsticks was all I could usually muster but just then I had remembered an old tune from way back when I was once a pair. Sterling and Strider made a good team and I hoped that my twin would remember that when we met toe to toe!

I scratched my head, "What was that tune Gabriel's dad would play on his toes with us socks on?" I asked myself.

Swag was sure to remember, I thought!

"Ah ha, I've got it!" I cried.

This little piggy went to Soxville!

Fluff and I burst into laughter; it was a very silly song but Gabriel loved it and secretly as did I and Strider. Gabriel would cry again, again, as we both hoped he would.

Suddenly, I had remembered the tune and before I knew it, I was busy playing the notes on the keyboard. We were too busy playing to notice that with every note played, a secret door

to the side opened a little further.

"I'm guessing that's our way in?" Fluff pointed out.

We moved slowly towards the opening and stepped through.

Chapter 13
THE HIDEOUT

Once inside the dimly lit cave we were led to a few steps, then onwards towards another hollow den. I did think that maybe we had made a mistake not waiting for the SBS socks to return, but, on reflection, maybe it was better I should catch my twin alone. I could at least just talk to him; either way I was here now, so I had best get on with it.

Suddenly, I could hear laughter, so we followed the sound. It was the chit chat of several so I knew we were definitely, well most probably, most likely to find the misfits.

My heart was beating out of my chest with excitement. This is it, I told myself, you have found Strider, aka Swag, and the misfits!

I approached with caution one step at a time; without warning, Sssirus appeared from nowhere.

"Gotcha, do you think we didn't know you were here?" Sssirus hissed!

Jigsaw had been entertaining the gang, joker of the misfits and by all accounts very funny. Once belonging to a comic book Monsters of Socks jigsaw, Sockinstein looked rather scary. "Looks can sometimes be deceiving,"

I chuckled. I was hoping Jigsaw had lightened the mood as I found myself standing there. I guess we were about to find out!

Coalstone Jack, a Welsh coal pirate, came to greet us.

"Iechyd da (Yaki da) butty bach, who do we have here then, now then?" he asked, hiccupping.

I had heard the rumour that Jack carried a vile of rum around his neck always, in honour of Captain Morgan. He never drunk himself, of course, but hiccupped a lot.

I was just about to introduce myself when a dark shadow came from behind the den.

"I know who this is! This is Sterling, my twin but not so alike!" Swag confirmed.

We just stood there looking at each other! I had dreamt of this moment for so long, but I was now lost for words.

"Let's not pussyfoot around, Sterling, we both know why you are here!" said Swag.

And of course, Swag was right! "Strider, let's talk," I suggested.

"I haven't been called Strider for a very long time; you may call me Swag!"

Swag ushered me into a room for some privacy. It seems we must have been talking for quite some time. Swag had explained that himself and the other misfits had been cast out of town for one reason and another and that, simply, they had just found each other.

I questioned why they were so disruptive in Soxville; his answer was not what I was expecting.

Swag went on to say that they only go into town to borrow items that they need and return them in good time.

"If that was true, then that would not explain why they are so afraid of you all!" I asked.

"We really are not sure about that? They simply run away from us! We shy away from the Soxville folk as much as we can!" Swag continued.

"Mmm, well I guess that's the mystery solved! Now maybe can we all get along? Hopefully, we can finally get back to King Hoof's palace and have that banquet I've been promised!" Fluff piped up, licking his lips.

Fluff was always thinking of his stomach!

"Oh, not so quick, what about the disappearance of the crown jewels? What about that?" I cried!

"No idea, it wasn't anything to do with us, was it? Lads!" Swag replied.

Looking around one by one, they all shook their heads signalling NO!

I did wonder if it was a little too convenient, but I had truly little else to go on; after all, their den was considerably basic with no evidence of luxury. I guess I had to take Swag's word for it and report back to base with our findings at Scotland Yarn HQ.

Swag had suggested that we take the short route back through Clog Woods. In no time at all we were holding a meeting with Sleuth Steele, Scissor and Stone!

A hundred miles an hour I blurted out the tales of our journey and the circumstances of Swag and the misfits.

Sleuth Steele was busy writing down notes whilst

Scissor and Stone listened intently.

I expressed that I believed that the misfits had been telling the truth and that I was happy to manage the situation with their agreement.

Just then General Smythe burst through the door!

"Ah, gentle socks, I'm glad I have found you all, I have some important news. I have received vital information regarding the crown jewels. Who? What? When? Why? I hear you ask!" General Smythe continued.

"I hadn't said a word!" Fluff whispered.

I was too nervous to laugh; General Smythe was a striking looking fellow who had a commanding charm about him.

"We are all ears, General, let me guess. Swag and the misfits again?" piped up Sleuth Steele!

I could feel the butterflies in my stomach fluttering around. I had so hoped that Swag was not involved, but suddenly this was looking more and more likely. I sat down with a heavy heart!

"It's OK, Sterling, we have each other whatever we hear!" assured Fluff.

"What, the misfits you say? Oh no, you got this all wrong!" replied General Smythe.

It turns out, after a proper search of the palace they found the crown jewels in the laundry basket! Yes, you heard right – the laundry basket! Was the funniest of things. Old footman Hobble thought it a good idea to give the jewels a good wash. Only problem was Hobble had forgotten to put them back and had been on holiday at the time of the search.

This was exceptionally good news; jumping up with delight we were back on track. All I had to do now was to convince the General and King Hoof that the misfits were not as bad as they thought!

I knew this was not going to be easy, but I had to give it a go!

Chapter 14
THE GREAT REVEAL

It was going to take some time to get Swag, the misfits and the Soxville folk to see eye to eye, but I was convinced that I was the right sock for the job.

I laid out a plan for a treaty in which both sides would be happy. The misfits would now be named the Seekers. They had only wanted to be treated the same as the town's folk; yes, they looked different with a few flaws, but no one is perfect, and we should all learn to accept each other. After all, everyone is unique in different ways!

My time in Soxville was coming to an end. You see, I am still a lucky sock and it is my duty to give as much luck as possible.

Fluff had fallen in love with Miss Lint, Grande Dame Darning's prodigy, so had decided to stay in Soxville.

As for Swag, who kept his name, I for one like it; it does have a certain cool ring to it!

So, you see, girls and boys, mums and dads, aunties and uncles, grandmas and grandpas alike, be kind, listen to each other – it will be more rewarding in the long run. Try to be patient, generous, fabulous and above all BE YOURSELF!

I am Gabriel's lucky sock, but I am also Agent Sterling Sox waiting for my next mission!

About the Author

Born in South Wales emigrated and educated in Vancouver Island, B.C, Canada in the eighties and currently resides in beautiful Carmarthenshire. Inspired by the curious minds and the fabulous vivid imagination's of the littlest of people. First time children's author, Lisa, loves to be creative and is currently working on her next book. In her spare time you will find her painting abstracts and no doubt searching for that elusive lost sock.

Acknowledgements

Thank you to my partner, Steve, for the encouragement not to give up on my dreams and for the love that shines my brightest light always. To my son, Joshua, who has always been my personal champion and who I am forever proud. To the Nicol clan who have always supported my quirky ways. I love you all.